SOURIA

Laird Ryan States

ISBN: 978-0-9940183-7-3

Cover is based on "Twin Beaches on a Small Island off the South-west Coast of
Selayar, South Sulawesi" by Fabio Achilli
The original image has been modified by the cover designer.
https://www.flickr.com/photos/travelourplanet/15001561159
It is used under the Creative Commons Attribution Licence
Cover designed by Ryan States
The poem "Sel Souris" was written by Rilla Friesen and is used with
permission
The drawing "Sketch of Indigene by Landers Somerset" is by Andrew
Postnikoff and used with permission
The song "Souria" was written and performed by Gayleen Froese. The lyrics
are printed with her permission
The song can be heard at
http://theasp.ca/wp-content/uploads/2016/06/Souria.mp3

With thanks and love to:

My mother, Nancy States
My real brother, Devon States
My Sister, Charla States
And my nephews Tristan and Taevon.

Family is hard, but worth it.

Also to

Gayleen Froese, as always
Rilla Friesen
Andrew Postnikoff

And to

Steven Angel, Kate Johnson, Sky Sorenson, and Tom Cantine
for their feedback and assistance.

And to

Hunter S. Thompson, William S. Burroughs, Philip José Farmer,
and Kurt Vonnegut

And to
The people of Sel Souris

And to
Niles Townsend, Carter Bennet, Tom Bradstreet, Victor
Mayhew,
and Carl Jherek

Sel Souris

they salted the earth before
fleeing their shame
beaten
beat
the beetles now claim the grave
psychedelic beetles
oilslicks of colour
millions of priests and prophets
of a dead race
they will not be crushed
so easily
delicate wings
still
mirthless faces
pale
the barren land
folds them to its breast
and the beetles swarm
they swarm

  -Rilla Friesen

Laird Ryan States

Souria

A hand span down, hot gone cold, you could almost believe you don't need the air that eats your cells and one day makes you old.

The river called while you were in there. It's been running around town all night looking for you. Did you dream in there? Did something move over your skin as a river would, turning bad debts good?

The island woke while you were in there. It sent spies through the woodwork looking for you. The river came in under my door. It filled every hollow reaching for you. The ocean drowned this building. It wore me to sand pushing to you.

The river called while you were in there. It's been running around town all night looking for you. The island woke. The river called.

Did you dream in there? Did something move under your skin?

-Gayleen Froese

The song can be heard at
http://theasp.ca/wp-content/uploads/2016/06/Souria.mp3

Table of Contents

INTRODUCTION

SEL SOURIS IS A SMALL island two hours away from Gibraltar by small plane. It has been traded between the colonial powers since being discovered in the late 16th century, not because it is desireable, but because it very much is not. It's populated by refugees and oddballs and castoffs from a wide variety of cultures, all of which have been uniquely transformed by the local ecology into a more or less tightly knit polyglot culture. The local ecology is sparse. Most, if not all of the flora was introduced by wind or the action of colonists. The fauna is almost entirely insectile. No large mammals seem ever to have been native to the island, and they don't tend to do well. Birds do not seem to like the place.

What Sel Souris has, in abundance, aside from salt, is a particular kind of iridescent purple beetle that swarms everywhere. The locals have found countless uses them. These uses are largely domestic, but there are a couple of notable uses for export as well.

Since the beginning of the twentieth century, no citizens of the former European colonial powers have been allowed to set foot on the island without serious consequences. In the mid-eighties, an English tourist snuck onto the island. He was blinded and sent home. This was something of a momentary media hubbub, but despite some saber rattling, nothing came of it. The powers that be want nothing at all to do with the island. It's more trouble to administer than they are likely to gain in reward. The locals will not be pacified.

Sel Souris has held a certain pull on artists and writers and musicians as well, since the century turned.

Laird Ryan States

William Burroughs was inspired by Sel Souris in his depiction of the Interzone in his writing Hunter S. Thompson,Timothy Leary, and Ken Kesey were all seekers after the rare drug called Purple Haze. It is found in abundance on the island, and is occasionally available, though expensive and hard to find, elsewhere. Jimi Hendrix, of course, wrote the song by that name inspired by his use of the drug, and its intense invocation of oneness with all things.

The Beatles, in fact, were originally known as The Purple Beatles, but the name was changed on the insistence of their agent and the record company. They wrote most of the Revolver album after taking heavy doses of Haze.

In the mid-seventies, Philip K Dick and Robert Anton Wilson experienced what they called "downloads" from alien intelligences after their experimentation with Purple Haze.

The late Prince Nelson was also a visitor to Sel Souris, and the song Purple Rain evokes not just the sense of oneness that Hendrix wrote of, but also the sense of sad dislocation that comes on users of Purple Haze when sobriety settles in, and the unity high fades away. His sense of fashion was inspired by the island, and many of his signature outfits were dyed using Sel Souris beetle by-products. He felt that he received a mild, constant contact high from this dye. He was likely right.

For my part, I feel a strong personal connection to the island.

Sel Souris is mentioned, at least in passing, in everything I've written since about 2005. I don't see that changing any time soon. Sel Souris is also one of the backbones of my personal magical practice. So, for a start, I'll get this out of the way. It was insufficiently flaky of me to be a writer, I had to go and become a magician as well.

As magicians go, I'm less flaky than most. I don't spurn modern science or medicine, especially medicine. I think Reiki, Chiropractic, Acupuncture, Homeopathy, and all their related ilk aren't just silly, but dangerous. I'm a rationalist, and I believe in the real world, and in things which are provable. I think that the increase in living standards and life expectancy show very clearly that science is the path forward.

I don't think magical thinking is a great way to run a society, and, in fact, I think it's pure mind poison for most people, letting them justify all manner of stupidity, bigotry, dogma, and hate. However, I think that it's a good idea to have a small number of practitioners in the world, exploring magic, pushing the limits of internal exploration, and seeking options. I don't think magic and rationality are at odds. At all.

The human brain is a complex machine, not built by design, but by committee. In this case, the committee is evolution. Evolution is a highy disorganized process. At the BEST of times, things designed by committee are often full of nooks and crannies and forgotten annexes that inform how they work but which cannot be fully understood.

Certain archetypes and concepts appear over and over, independently in the practice of magic irrespective of cultural influence. Shamanistic beliefs, in particular, share some shocking commonalities seeming to spring up from the depths of the human consciousness independently all over the world.

In my opinion, magic is the practice of getting to the underlying code of the human brain. When I speak to spirits, I am speaking to certain archetypical structures and processes that lie within each human mind. There are ways to access information and opinions kept from your conscious mind, and to dramatically, if temporarily, alter your own perceptions and attitudes.

I don't think that it's any kind of accident, that a central tenet of magic worldwide is the idea that your own ego, your own identity is your biggest obstacle in accessing the power of magic. I think it's essential, because the idea of magic is to talk to your brain directly and get your personality out of the way.

Of course, this is just my opinion, and I could be wrong. Any two practitioners of magic who agree absolutely on how it works, and how it is best used, are probably kidding themselves.

I do not believe in the objective reality of the spirits I speak to, and that is essential to my practice. I think that when I speak to the gods, I'm speaking to my own deep mind, I'm accessing wisdom locked away in a brain that works overtime, that has ways of approaching perception I no longer commonly use.

And it would be easy for me to dismiss the supernatural entirely. I wish that I could. I am sure that ninety percent of the time, my own biases, confirmation and otherwise, have deceived me most of the time as to any real world effects my magical practice has wrought. I am not confident that's all there is to it, though.

For example: I have done group workings, asking for the assistance of people on the internet to achieve particular goals. These seem to ALWAYS work. I don't know why. Luck, perhaps? But it feels like something real.

For example: I buy a scratch lottery ticket once a week, as part of a long term arrangement with my primary patron, Ganesha. I am $135 dollars up on those tickets. Statistically, these are much luckier for me than they have any reason to be. It's not big money, but I rarely lose. I rarely fail to recoup my weekly cost. I know this is not usual. I can't explain it. Luck perhaps.

I have seen spirits move things on a few occasions. I have seen physical effects on the world worked by spirits. I have no explanation for this. Self-deception? Maybe. I don't know.

Magic is weird. It is EXACTLY that which is not sensible. And, for me, above all else, it's about what works.

What does this have to do with the pieces you have at hand? Well. Sel Souris is a kind of experiment. I decided to believe in the island, in defiance of all fact to the contrary.. I decided that other people should too—not consciously, perhaps—for it's not a place that can be easily believed in, but to pull that trick I pull on myself when I am doing magic, to blur that line. To cause that instant of doubt and dissonance that IS magic for me.

Philip José Farmer did this for me with his books Tarzan Alive and Doc Savage: His Apocalyptic Life. I knew that these characters could not be real, that they did not exist in the real world. He pretended so hard, and so well, that I did have that MOMENT of doubt, that few seconds of possibility. This was the beginning of magic for me.

And, to me, the place is real. And every once in a while, I receive some small evidence from other people that it is for them as well.

Souria is a collection of two of the earliest pieces I wrote about my experience with Sel Souris, and while I think they are kind of rough in spots, they have a freshness and a spark of magic in them that makes me love them and want to share them, in spite of their flaws.

This is raw stuff, spat out by a writer ten years younger than I am, without a lot of my present hesitations, and with great enthusiasm. I've tightened them up a bit, but I have left them, in essence, as they were.

Friends and online acquaintances have seen versions of these in the past. To others they'll be new.

They don't fit with the rest of my work these days, I'm never going to be able to recycle them into longer manuscripts. They don't really stand on their own enough to submit to the short fiction market.

This is the kind of thing that electronic self publishing was made for. I can economically publish them, and so here I am, doing that.

I can't pretend these are perfect. I do love them, though, as I love VERY few things I wrote so long ago. I hope you derive some pleasure from them. I can tell you one thing, for sure: You're getting a more direct view into my head with these than you will with most of what I write.

Thanks for buying, and thanks for reading.

Laird Ryan States—June 12, 2016

Laird Ryan States

FEAR AND LOATHING

THIS PIECE CAME TO ME very shortly after the Sel Souris project began. It is, in essence, a direct relation of a dream I had. After verbally relating the dream to a few people, I decided to capture it on paper. Reading it now, so many years later, it still amuses me. My take on Thompson is spotty, but I like the story, and I am surprised to see how many little details of the story inform my later work. Also, it's a piece of straight up comic fiction. I don't think I've ever written one before or since. This is a missive from my hindbrain, informed by my influences and idols. I am proud I venerate my gods a little less respectfully than most.

Fucking beetles! Thousands upon endless thousands of the little fuckers swarm & roil over everything like maggots on a day old corpse. It's the summer season on Sel Souris & we're told by the woman behind the desk at the hotel that in summer the beetles breed out of control here

"Where are all the fucking birds?" I ask her, clenching my teeth down on my cigarette holder & looking at her while an officious little prick named Jherek translates for me. She says something back & Jherek interprets, telling me there are no birds on the island.

"That's fucking preposterous," I say. My guide doesn't bother translating. He looks at me with a barely disguised look of contempt. I'm the ugly American to him, which is deeply insulting but what can you expect of a fucking barbarian.

"The beetles are why you came, Mr. Duke," he says, with a smarmy little smile like that clever little asshole in the second grade who reminds the teacher about the homework.

"The hell they are. I came to get bombed out of my skull on the rarest & most delicate of narcotics," I say. "And, of course, to see the beautiful local scenery."

As scenery goes, it isn't bad. The island is green & not covered over with asphalt & wiring, yet. The town itself though is run down in a vaguely appealing way. Animals run through the streets here & all the buildings are painted in shades of pink & purple & white & it's all a little queasy at this time of the day. It has the usual third world smells, both good & bad. The people gabble at one another in what they pretend is a language, but which is actually just a noise they use to distract from the elaborate code of tics & gestures by which they secretly conspire to bilk me of drugs & money.

"Yes," Jherek says, "And so you shall."

"I need a drink," I say, turning on my heel & heading up to my room.

The room is the same pastel pink as everything else. There is a table & on the table I had already laid out the tools of my trade, the trusty portable Underwood on which I capture these words & a 9 mm Browning pistol, gleaming in the early afternoon sun & still smelling of gun oil. You can never be sure which will be of more use in a place like this.

Sel Souris is one of the bad crazy places left over from 200 years of Europe fucking the third world in the ass with the dildo of colonialism. The people here are remnants & rejects of the European hegemony, clinging to this broken little chunk of rock, as indestructible as cockroaches & twice as nasty. They hate the world & anyone who wasn't born here, but they need our money & they want to be taken seriously as a country. As if that's something to be proud of. Nobody cares about this place but the crazy & the wrecked & the pilgrims looking to blow their minds with the substance known popularly as Purple Haze, thought by most to be a fiction, but in actuality only rare & expensive.

It might be the only place in the world where, once you live there, you can do as you like.

What they call a constitution on this godforsaken rock is little more than a series of angry threats. I ought to love it here. It's the world's first gonzo country. I don't love it. I fucking hate it & as soon as I'm done this article, I'll leave & I'll never think of it again except in bad dreams & flashbacks.

I can't stand the noise of the goats in the streets & so I pull out the battery operated cassette player from my suitcase & play The Rolling Stones loudly. I lay on the bed & try to ignore the beetles that crawl over me. It's not the first time I've used this skill & there's no reason it should be any harder when they're real.

I am nearly in the place where sleep can strike me on the back of the skull & drag me down into the deep heaviness of the barbiturated void when there is a pounding on the wall of my room. For a moment, I am convinced I am back in Saigon & that I'm being shot at. I sit stock upright in bed, sweating, Sympathy For The Devil is playing & I hear the crotchety indistinct rumbling of the lunatic in the room next door.

I put my gun in the back of my slacks & I go out into the hall & hammer on the door, demanding, in formal but insulting verbiage, that the lunatic miscreant show himself. I am astonished when the door swings open & I find myself face to face with the famous junkie writer William Lee. Emotions trample me like a herd of swine, no two headed the same way. This man before me is a trailblazer, my literary antecedent, many would say & certainly a man of talent & breeding.

"Turn off that fucking nigger music," he says with an angry smile. a revolver in his right hand, a cane in the other.

"Bill?" I say, astonished, "Are you really here on this island, or are you an hallucination. You can confide in me."

He looks at me evenly.

"I'm an old man," he says. "Turn that shit off."

I stumble over myself to turn off the music & I come back out to the hall, where he is still standing.

"Now answer my question," I say, an edge in my voice.

"Raoul Duke," he says, his deep Southern voice a dessicated snarl, "You are terminally fucked up. You are a danger to yourself & other people. You should be locked up."

"Naturally," I say, "Without question. What brings you to Sel Souris?"

"The same thing as you, I expect," he says, "Narcotics & the libertarian urge."

"Have you tried it then? Have you had Purple Haze?"

"Don't call it that, for Christ's sake," he says, "People here call it 'the beetle'."

"Why the fuck do they call it that?"

He sneers a tired southern sneer & pushes his cane through a cluster of big purple beetles, smearing their guts on the floor.

"When life gives you lemons, make lemonade," he says with a raspy chuckle.

"That's vile," I say, "Unspeakably so. I've taken adrenochrome, distilled from the stolen adrenal glands of Nicaraguan prostitutes & I still think that's worse."

He shrugged.

"I don't think it's for you," Bill says, "not to your taste."

"I'll be the judge of that!"

"Doubtless," he says & moves to close the door.

I stand there in the naked contempt of that gesture & I wonder why I was surprised. It's the drugs, I think. I should have known I might see him here. He's been to the island more times than any American of note, they say, back to when he was a young man. You can see it in his writing, insectile & disjointed, just like this place & brilliant in a decay & loam kind of way, also like this place.

I go back to my room & sleep a while to the soft whispering of hard shell on hard shell. I wake up with a feeling that leaves me queasy & shaking. They call this sensation sobriety & I swallow a handful of red pills with some of the local beer. It tastes like dirt, but my teeth are soon pointy & I keep thinking more & more about Lee the longer I sit here. The burned-out old faggot junkie treating me like some kind of reprobate trash fills me with a dangerous anger.

I storm into his room & I throw my typewriter on the wooden desk beside his own. His typewriter rears & flattens its platen with deep hostility.

"What the hell are you doing, you maniac," Lee yells at me, "They'll tear each other apart."

"What are you frightened your bird can't keep up?" I snap back, as my Underwood rears back, clicking its spacebar in challenge.

"The hell I am," Lee responded. "Why don't we make it interesting?"

In a flash we have pulled our tools away from each other & slipped the long steel barbs onto them & we set them on the floor where they alternately rush & back away before they fall on each other clacking & ringing in a fight to the death. We each cheer our own on, as keys clatter & are pecked to the floor. The commotion summons passersby who cheer & exchange dollar bills in betting until at last both combatants slump in a mutual tangle of red & black ribbon.

"I'll be goddamned," I say, "It's been known to happen from time to time, but I've never seen a fight with no survivors like that. I admit it, Bill, you've won my respect. Your bird could fight."

He nods & shakes my hand, but this moment of reconciliation is cut short. The crowd has turned ugly. Nobody knows who to call the winner. The people holding the money are reluctant to return it & angry words are being thrown about. I decide to get out of there before the mob tears me apart like hungry vultures.

I close the door to my room, lucky to be alive & proceed to capture the experience longhand until I once again pass out.

I wake up an hour or two later as the sun is going low in the sky. Some thoughtful fellow has replaced my torn & broken Underwood with a nearly identical model. They have seen fit, also, to type up the hand-written notes I left. This was probably the work of a grateful local who won big in the affair next door. Damned fine thing to do, though I worry about the security of the room & if he could still be inside. I search & find nothing but beetles everyplace.

I decide that I'm hungry & I head out into the hall & down to the lobby. Lee is speaking in Arabic to an old man by the window.

"Bill," I say, "Let me buy you lunch. It's the least I can do, considering the mayhem in your room & the loss of your tool."

He looks at the old man, as if he might have understood me better & getting nothing from him, turns back to me.

"I don't have the slightest idea what you're talking about, you degenerate fool."

I laugh & pull him up to his feet & he strikes me slightly with the head of his cane.

"Don't put your hands on me. I don't want to get any on me."

I step back still grinning, but a hint of something else filtering through me.

"Hey," I say, "come on. I'm trying to make it up to you here. We're both decent men & we share a trade for Christ's sake."

"You balding half-witted barbary ape," Lee growls at me, "I'd sooner eat with Nixon than sit at your table."

I lose my temper, feeling the amphetamine reminiscent rush of adrenaline.

"Who the hell do you think you are, old man? Do you know who I am? I'm Raoul Duke. You don't get to talk to me like that."

"I'll talk to you any goddamned way I choose."

I shoot him a lethal glare.

"This isn't lawful territory," I say, "so you might want to consider carefully how to talk to an armed man."

Lee laughs, barking like a hyena & he reaches up from his chair & slaps my face.

"I demand satisfaction," he says.

My eyes roll around in my head as I try to piece his words into some human language.

"Did you just challenge me to a gunfight?"

"Tomorrow at sunrise," Lee says. "Unless you'd care to apologize & then to leave me the hell alone. I'm trying to have a vacation."

"The hell I'll apologize to you. I'm just a man trying to make up for killing your typewriter. I lost a good one myself you know!"

He shakes his head.

"I'll see you in the morning then," he says, "Bring your second, if you can find one. We'll start back to back, then ten paces & fire. Then I'll have breakfast while they feed you to their pigs."

I blink, feeling two steps behind & then to preserve my dignity, I turn & walk away nodding.

If this conversation had happened in the civilized world I'd have assumed we were kidding, but we aren't in the civilized world. And I've been called out for an honest to god duel by arguably the finest writer in the world & the grandfather of gonzo himself & I'm okay with that because in person he has turned out to be a total prick. If he wants me to shoot him, then I'll shoot him full of holes & be famous for just one more reason.

It's then that fear hits me in the gut & I realize that I have agreed to something unbelievably fucked up & dangerous. One of the things Lee is famous for is missing an apple & shooting his wife in her face at a party. This doesn't speak well to his aim, but it means he's already taken a life, something which I, in all my bluster, can't claim.

And if the magazines are right, his aim has improved & I imagine I might have gone the same road, not wanting to let THAT happen to me again, fuck no.

I'm not hungry anymore & I wander upstairs to think about this. What I need is a strategy. If my attorney were here I'd ask his advice, but he is trapped back in the world dealing with his own shit & I am on my own. I pace the floor like a trapped animal, burning myself up with pills & whiskey & trying to get some kind of clarity.

I go for a walk through the town, ignoring the idiot stares of the locals acting like they never saw a real person before. On the way back to the hotel I am propositioned by a woman who thinks she is a whore, but I can't imagine there's much call for her here & I prefer real professionals & besides which I'm a married man.

Jherek is outside my hotel when I get back, impatient & insolent & he snaps at me.

"I've been waiting for two hours for you," he says. "I should kill you."

"There's no need," I say, "Smart money is on me dying at sunrise. Did you bring the drugs?"

He nods & hands me a small silk pouch filled with a glittering purple powder. It smells like figs & coffee & everything exotic & I want to inject it directly into my brain at once. I hand him the money & go up to my room. I lay out several lines of it & inhale it quickly.

Immediately, I feel my spine liquefy. I can look at my hands & see them floating there at the end of me, but they might as well belong to someone else for all the connection I feel to them.

I am pissed off now because Lee is right. I don't like this kind of soft pussy oneness high. I hear the blood in my ears & the ghost of a heartbeat with which my own synchronizes & for the better part of forever I lay paralyzed in purple warmth that is like nothing else I've put in my body. I don't remember much of it.

When I come out of it I take four blacks & swallow them with vodka & I feel a little less strange & a little more like a stranger. Never again with that purple voodoo. I'll leave that to the hippies & Aquarians. I prefer this feeling, aware & awake & every second is so precious that I know I can't let myself die.

I come to a brilliant plan. I will turn on 8 & shoot Lee in the back. It isn't honorable, but then neither is death. I could run back to the mainland, but I'm a whore for fame & I can't think of any faster way to get more than to kill my literary father like a speed freak Oedipus.

I repeat it in my head over & over like a mantra. Turn on 8 & fire, over & over I say it to myself trying to train myself so I can't possibly forget & wind up dead.

In the morning I am out front of the hotel before dawn. I am alone, bringing no second, & needing none. I am the lone wolf & seconds are for old men who are afraid of things. I am stone cold & bulletproof as I wait. Word has spread, apparently, as people know Bill here & it's not a big place. I'm not surprised a crowd should turn up.

In Sel Souris, duelling, like everything else, is legal but frowned upon. The sour faced locals line the streets. A murmur goes through the crowd & William Lee makes his appearance coming out of the hotel in his brown suit & his brown fedora carrying his ancient revolver.

It's huge, his gun, but primitive & I think to myself that my gun is smaller & faster & meaner. Our guns tell the whole story.

"All right," he says, "you inveterate cocksucker, let's get this over with."

His second takes his coat from him & Lee looks so thin & old, I almost feel ashamed about shooting him.

We stand back to back & his second starts to count us off, his accent atrocious but understandable & we know the lines.

"One," he says & we take a step. Turn on 8 & shoot, I tell myself.

"Two," the kid says & we step. Turn on 8, I tell myself & I feel fear sweat on the back of my neck.

"Three."

I hear Lee cough. I remind myself to turn on 8 & fire.

"Four."

There is a shot that cracks the morning air & I see my own belly, spray blood out on to the dirt. I stare at the blood spreading out on my shirt, & my knees give way as I drop to the dirt, too breathless to properly scream. I hear a choke in the back of my throat. I feel my life trickling between my fingers.

There is no sound from the people watching & I roll over to see Lee calmly putting his suit coat on.

"You all saw it," he says. "I had no choice. I had to shoot. Son of a bitch pulled a gun on me."

His second translates, yelling it out & the people laugh their guts out as I bleed in the dirt, beetles crawling over me until I gratefully, mercifully, pass the fuck out.

THE IRRESPONSIBLE JOURNEY

THIS PIECE WAS WRITTEN OVER a period of several days in December of 2006 on a long defunct blog called The Rook's Nest. It came without preface or planning, and was my first major work of false document writing. I had assumed that people would very quickly twig to this being a piece of fiction, that I was, in fact, fictionalizing my life, for the sole purpose of trying to reach Sel Souris. I was, in essence, building myself a rocket to shoot into fictional space and interact with my creation. Most did get it. Those who didn't were uncertain if I had simply slipped a cog, or what. A few people got really mad at me. I regret nothing. The responses I got were, aside from some few angry folks, uniformly positive.

For my part, this was a ritual, and that ritual was successful. It ends, I think, rather less well than it starts, but I'm fond of this piece anyway, and it was the beginning of a real change in how I worked. This is writing about writing, disguised as a fictional travelogue.

And I still have days when I deeply miss the part of my family you meet in this story. I feel a legitimate ache when I remember the smells of them, and the expressions on their faces.

Real is a funny word.

How far can a credit card take you?

I applied for a visa three years ago, and got a call TODAY from the travel bureau that I was cleared to visit as of immediately. I dropped everything, and I mean everything, packed my bags, and took a cab to the airport.

I touched down in Sel Souris about two hours ago.

From the landing strip, I caught a ride (not for free, I can tell you) to my hotel. Everything is unspeakably strange, and for a change I don't understand a single solitary word that anybody says here. There are no snatches of French, which has been illegal here since the end of the First World War. There are no snatches of Spanish or German or any of the languages I at least would recognize. There is a sort of English spoken here for the benefit of tourists, but I am missing a lot of it. They speak it too fast, and the accent is somewhere between Eastern Europe and Arabia. Which is, of course, what you'd expect.

The people here are not warm or friendly. It's all business. They don't like North Americans. They don't actually like anyone, as near as I can tell, not even each other. It's a lot of lean angular faces, pale grey people in stark contrast with the fashions here. My god, the colours—peacock colours, shades of blue and rich purples and pale almost frosted pinks. Everybody wears them, young or old, regardless of gender.

Sel Souris is not a large place. It consists of one small island that tapers at the southern tip to a long thread of a peninsula. The entire place is not much bigger than Monaco, and is getting a little smaller each year as the ocean levels rise. Were it an independent country, it would be a footnote country, notable for its tiny size, much as Monaco and Lichtenstein are known for this.

Sel Souris is not an independent country, though it claims sovereignty. It is, technically, at the moment, a Belgian Protectorate. Belgium disputes responsibility with France, neither wanting to officially claim it. The population of Sel Souris wants nothing to do with either.

The population of the island is guessed to be somewhere around 1100 people, though there is no census. The economy is service based, and the American dollar and the Swiss franc are used here with equal commonality.

The government, what there is of it, consists of a sort of rotating mob of police and soldiers that enforce the Constitution of Sel Souris. It's not a very lengthy document.

It's not easy to visit Sel Souris. At present they accept tourists on two-day visas and only from Canada, the United States of America, Australia, and Japan. Europeans are not allowed. Sel Souris made the news fifteen years ago when a British tourist faked his way onto the island with a Canadian passport and was blinded and deported. You may recall, but I doubt it. The world likes to forget about everything that happens on this island. It's understandable.

Why am I in Sel Souris? A lot of reasons. I've been fascinated with the place since I was 7 years old. It was the name at first, but eventually I started to learn about the history of the island, and exactly why the West doesn't talk about it.

There's another reason though. I have a half brother who lives here. We've never met, maybe shared a half dozen quick phone calls, and some extensive letters. He's the real reason I'm here. We're going to meet face to face for the first time, and together I hope we can head out all the way to the tip of the peninsula, and see what I came here to see. It's the wreck of what just might be an alien spacecraft, or what might be something even more important than that.

It's a long story, and to be honest, I'm exhausted. I had no intention of leaving the country today, and yet here I am.

I'll touch base tomorrow.

Holy shit

Hi, I'm at my brother's place this morning. It's late, or early, depending on your reckoning. His internet connection is better than the one at the hotel was. I need to hit the sheets in the worst way possible, but I also needed to touch base. I know that some people are a little concerned. I got a rather long email from a person who I've talked to about this place and she was worried that I'd left so impulsively.

Let me tell you, I'm fine. I'm better than fine.

It's going to probably take me weeks to tell you everything that happened today. I am seriously going to need a few days to process this.

Laird Ryan States

Have you ever noticed that sometimes more happens to you in a single day than you can even believe? The sheer amount of exotic data today has left me fucking baffled.

I have never left Canada in my life before yesterday. I've never so much as visited the States for fuck's sake. Today I'm sleeping in the house of a brother I've never met, half way around the world, in a house on the southernmost tip of an island so obscure that, in my life, I've only met four people who've even heard of it. I'm sleeping less than a mile from the strangest thing on earth, in my opinion. I've touched it.

So forgive me for not spilling forth the details right away. I need to wrap my own head around it first.

I do have one thing to say though. Two things. First of all, I am not at all comfortable riding in rickshaws. I'm pretty sure what I rode earlier today wasn't what is traditionally called a rickshaw, but it was close. It was a single man carriage with two wheels. It's pulled by four men, teenagers in this case, each at the end of a long pole on either side of the carriage. Three motivate the thing, while the fourth rests for ten minutes, and they swap off in turns. Nice kids, and they seemed to enjoy working together. I'm not comfortable with it. I am also not comfortable with being considered rich. Especially because I am pretty much positive I will be paying this trip off for the next fifteen fucking years at 19% interest. I don't care. Worth it. So worth it.

Second thing, my brother here is tall and thin and good looking, just like the brother I grew up with. Fuck you genetics. Not fair. But his daughter is turning 14 in a week and she is just as pretty as he is, so he'll suffer. Heh.

I catch a plane out of here late tomorrow, or, I suppose, today now and should be back home by Wednesday at the latest. I'm not in the same ass busting rush to get home that I was to get here. I wonder if I will be fired when I get back.

I don't think fucking off to follow a dream is considered an acceptable excuse for missing work.

Lucky I live in Alberta.

Jet lag

I am home. It is fucking cold here.

Don't ever let anyone tell you New York is the greatest city in the world. It's a fucking hellhole, and the air tastes like a fat man's sweaty armpits, only he is on fire.

I will start recounting my trip shortly. Right now I want a bath, and some food that doesn't have any fish in it.

I am, happily, not fired. This is especially good in light of the fact that I am now indebted to a degree that is purely terrifying. Read on, to see how I ruined my financial life.

Saturday morning: 5:40 am

The phone rings. I am less horrified than you might expect because I am up anyway. I have signed on for overtime this morning at work. I am in a hurry only because I don't wish to have G wake up.

"Hello," I say, mildly annoyed.

"Is this Ryan States?"

"Yes," I say, more annoyed. The faint hiss on the line and the Oxford English with a hint of something exotic makes me think it's a telemarketer outsourced to India.

"I am Carl Jherek from the Sel Souris travel commission."

"What?"

"I am sorry," he says, "bad connection. I am from Sel Souris travel commission."

"Really?"

"Yes. Your application for visiting privileges has been reviewed and accepted based on the recommendation and bond posted by your brother Landers Somerset."

"Thank you," I say, barely able to stand up. I did not expect to hear from this committee. Not ever.

"You are cleared to stay 48 hours in Sel Souris, or slightly longer if travel conditions are not ideal. Application may be made on arrival for extension."

"How soon am I allowed to visit? Do I have to wait for the April window?"

I hear a smile on his voice. He's pleased that I know about their typical tourist policies. I've earned points, and this pleases me.

"No. The bond posted by your brother allows you to come at will."

"How much notice do you require. I have to make arrangements."

"Twelve hours is sufficient. There are papers to sign when you arrive."

I get the number to call, and he also provides me with an email address. I am surprised, pleasantly about that.

I decide to call in sick to work. I pace the house like a nut for two hours, packing, finding my passport. I have kept my passport current since I turned 18. You never know when the country you're in will take a dark fucking turn.

I check my credit cards. A recent credit limit increase on all three of them has left me with enough credit that I can do this. I shouldn't. I really shouldn't. I will though, there's no question at all. I want to meet Landers. I want to see the peninsula, and what lies at the tip.

It is 8 am, and I begin to call travel agents. It takes 7 calls before I find one who knows where the place is. She quietly asks me if I have approval. I say yes. She asks for the number of my travel visa. I tell her I will have to call her back.

I call the island and after ten minutes I get my number.

I call her back. I give it to her. She says she needs to make some calls and will call me back.

Gayleen wakes up. I tell her my visa has been approved. She asks what visa I'm talking about. I tell her. She informs me that the island was on the 10 most dangerous places in the world to visit according to Danger Finder.

We don't talk about it for a few minutes. The phone rings, and the agent asks me how soon I want to be there. I tell her that I'd like to go as soon as humanly possible. I hear her typing and clicking. She comes back to me with a price. I nearly faint.

I say to the travel agent that I can't quite afford to be there that fast. She laughs.

She asks me to hold and I hold for a few minutes.

G looks at me, realizing that I am booking travel plans and stares at me the same way she often stares at Spenser. Spenser is five months old, and is a dog. What is my excuse? Whimsy.

The agent comes back online and asks me if I'd be willing to fly courier. I ask what that means. She explains the whole thing to me. Long story short, sometimes the major courier companies find it cheaper to send their packages as passenger cargo because it is so much faster to get it through customs that way.

The catch is that there must be an actual passenger in the seat. Apparently you can get some crazy deals. I tell her I would love that. She comes back to me with a price that is still very painful, but the most painful part of it BY FAR is the single engine small aircraft that will pick me up in Gibraltar and fly me to the island proper. The trip home, she can arrange courier for me, but I will have to stop in NYC and Minneapolis. That's fine with me as well.

The major catch for me is that I need to catch a plane to Calgary in ninety minutes. From there to Madrid, and then to Gibraltar. From there a chartered flight to Sel Souris.

G and I have the sort of talk that you'd expect we'd have, but I am in too much of a hurry for it to last long. She wants nothing to do with this, does not approve of this decision, and is worried. I let her know that I understand this, pet the dogs, hug her goodbye and step into a taxi. I make my flight by inches.

I have never been on a plane in living memory. I was on one flight when I was five. All I remember is the stewardess bending down to greet me. A pale washed out Kodak memory of a memory of a memory.

It is not pleasant. I feel that weird pre cold sniffly feeling from the canned air. The first flight is over very quickly, and I have to boot it to make the next one.

Three hours into a 7 hour flight, I take walks until the hostesses start trying not to be snippy. Everything feels swollen.

I change planes in England (hello England, I hear you are where some of my people came from. Welcome to my blog). I sleep my way to Madrid (hello Madrid, I hear you like bullfighting. Welcome to my blog)

I end up in Gibraltar, it's the middle of the night, and I am waiting for a plane. I am now half way around the world. I have no clear idea what day it is. I am cold, and the ocean is more fucking terrifying than I ever dreamed.

Laird Ryan States

I call my brother Landers. I tell him where I am, and he nearly dies laughing. It occurs to me that I had not called him until now. He doesn't seem angry. He would meet me at the airstrip except it is very early and his wife would skin him. He arranges a pickup for me there with a local taxi driver he says will be fair to me.

I hear the sound of an engine and I see the plane, dangerously old looking coming in across the water, and I say I have to go.

The plane circles in and comes for a landing. My bag is on my shoulder, my ID is strapped to me, and I am about to go to the strangest place in the world.

Everything is already so surreal that I wonder what impact it will have. The sun is coming up.

Tomorrow, the story of my other brother, Landers, my arrival in Sel Souris, and why I have no pictures of the trip.

Exposition

In order for the rest of this story to make any sense emotionally, I need to lay out some backstory for you about my life and heritage.

It comes as a shock to many people who meet my father to discover that he is black. I, after all, am very white indeed. That took some getting used to in childhood, people's shock I mean, because to me it's first nature. He's the only father I've ever known. He is not, of course, my biological father. My biological father is named Walter Somerset. He left my Mom in the middle of the night just before my second birthday leaving her twenty year old self a single mother with no means of support in 1973. He is, as I'm sure you've inferred, a peach.

I went through the whole wanting to meet my biological father phase in childhood. I said and did hurtful things to my adoptive father that I deeply regret. I was, in my defense, ten years old. Even at that age I had sussed out this much about my biological father: he was a fucking loser.

He also had an ongoing history of getting married, and bolting while the kid was in infancy. He's done it a lot since then. To be honest, I don't have a solid figure. I don't keep tabs on the man. He may be dead. I don't wish that or anything. It's just the truth that I don't know.

I have any number of half siblings out there. I don't know how many. My mother was in touch with one or two of his exes for a while. I don't ask. I've never looked them up. I'm basically not interested. My mother married my father, who adopted me, and this is my family now warts and all. I love them. I have a brother who is the light coffee colour you'd expect, and a half Chinese, half Cree sister we adopted. Our family is the thing of nightmare to those lackwits who fear "race mixing" whatever the hell that even means.

Sure, for a while, I thought it might be interesting to track them down, and see what we have in common, but I never took the step because, frankly, the one thing we all have in common is that our father, our biological father at least, is a shit. That doesn't seem like much of a foundation upon which to build.

Not all of us have been inclined not to look. About five years ago I received an email from a Landers Somerset. This immediately gained my interest because until I was five my last name was Somerset as well. I wondered if, god willing, I had inherited some vast fortune.

It turns out that I had, but not in the way I'd thought. Landers had first seen my work back in the days when I was running my first abortive attempt at a website called "And How!". He had done some looking into his father, our father, and he had run across my name. I have the questionable privilege of being his first child, and this makes me relatively easy to find through the old-fashioned channels. Nobody uses those anymore, they use the internet. A search for me on the web, though, if you haven't tried, will lead you nowhere. My name is a simple and common declarative phrase. Google me. Go on.

So, it was rather surprising when he found me, even to him. His first email was very polite, asking if I was who he thought I was. I wrote him back, kind of awkwardly, to explain I was, but that I really didn't have any attachment or interest in my biological father. I tried not to be offensive about it.

He wrote back, and I wish I had a copy of the email, but it was lost in one of the great hard drive crashes that plague our

23

age, and ensure that "The Complete Correspondence of Lucy Lunchbox (1970-2050)" is a book that will never see publication.

The long and the short of it was that he was trying to contact all of Walt's children because he had been diagnosed with Huntington's Disease, and he wanted to let the rest of us know about it. He then went on to ask me about the website and my writing, and mentioned that he too had little interest in expanding his family, but that he enjoyed what I was doing, and wanted to stay in touch.

Now, here is a thing that most people probably don't realize about me. I think that the sort of person who goes to the effort of tracking down a total stranger to let him know he might have the gene for Huntington's, simply because he feels it is his responsibility to do so, is a fucking hero.

Before I continue, it does not seem I have the gene for the disease. There is no cause for alarm.

Landers had earned my friendship, instantly. I wrote him back right away, and he wrote me back, and we talked about our lives. I don't want to go into all of it here, because Landers is a private person, and while he is also funny and warm, he is kind of shy. He would prefer I didn't go into all that much detail about him. Within three or four exchanges, we had traded addresses.

I remember very clearly the afternoon I got that email. I opened it, and read it six or seven times. Landers Somerset lived in Sel Souris. Sel Souris, as I've mentioned seemed barely real to me, like something out of a dream. My first exposure to it was in a book on the "unexplained". I ate those up as a kid, bigfoot photos, the Loch Ness Monster, UFOs, that sort of stuff. This book, the name of which escapes me now, though I know Ivan Sanderson was one of the authors, held a peculiar fascination for me because it held a photo that is burned into my memory. This photo, taken, from the looks of it, in the 19th century showed a pterodactyl nailed to a barn, the wingspan covering the entire side of the building, head lolling limply, and no fewer than twenty hunters posed in front, some standing and some kneeling. That photo held such mystery because it was so real, so clearly not retouched, and yet impossible. How could such a thing have not made international news. Yet there it was. I wish I still had the book. In that same book was an article on Sel Souris, which the authors said was "the strangest place on earth". The description of the island's history and inhabitants was very brief, but enough to keep me obsessed through childhood for any tidbits of knowledge I could find.

The thrust of the history, some of which was in the book, and thus is greatly oversimplified, is this: In 1751 a great flash of light was seen from the shores of Gibraltar, and a great stone was seen to splash into the water. When a ship went out to look for the object less than a day later, the island of Sel Souris, then unnamed was accidentally discovered. The discoverers were astonished because it is a relatively large island to have gone unnoticed.

The island was devoid of vegetation, and the only form of life they found were a great many brightly coloured beetles. Within ten years the island was populated by a number of colonists who introduced plant and animal life to the rock. Within fifteen, all the colonists there were dead of a "wasting plague". The island was considered unsuitable for colonisation for years and years. Ownership of the island bounced from nation to nation, ending up with the French, and nobody paid it any attention until 1830 when a Dutch trading ship ran aground on the island in a storm, to find the place populated by a mixed race agglomeration of inhabitants. The traders discovered two things there as well. First was that the northern and southern ends of the island were rich in salt. The second was that the locals produced a number of extremely vivid dyes from the ground carapaces of the beetles that swarmed there in abundance.

Word reached the French, who immediately installed a governor, and who named the island Sel Souris, in reference to the shape of the island, which, with the long tapering southern peninsula, did resemble a mouse somewhat. The salt at the head and tail of this mouse completed the image.

To the present day, I have no idea what the locals had called the place prior to the arrival of the French. I also don't know where the inhabitants came from. Nobody else does either. The island is a sort of reverse Roanoke. Instead of a whole town vanishing mysteriously and in a hurry, in this case a colony sprung from nowhere.

This in itself would be enough to make it the strangest place on earth. The final touch to the history, as the book relayed it, and this as an afterthought is that it is believed by some, including the locals, that the tail of Sel Souris is sediment covering the remains of a vessel from another world, a plague ship full of castaways. There the article ended, with no further comment or explanation.

In the twenty years or so that followed I found out precious little else about it. There are reasons for this. It's a pretty small and obscure place, first of all. With a history that weird, though, you'd think you'd hear more. I think, though it's not a conspiracy theory, to be clear, that Europe tries awfully hard to look away from Sel Souris because the island is at the center of a very shameful part of history. I'll talk more about that when I talk about my time there.

I'm straddling a fine line between telling the whole story in a chaotic lump and just giving you what you need to follow the story of my trip.

So, to drag us back from the flashback within the exposition, I stared at his address unbelieving.

I sent him an email asking if he was kidding. He told me he was not. He's an entomologist, and his specialty is in beetles. The beetles of Sel Souris are very interesting, and while he was there back in University, he met a local woman there, got her pregnant and married young. Now he's what passes for a citizen there. It's like any other island though, he's not part of the real community. He explained he lives out on the tail, which is a bit removed from Sel Souris, the town. He studies the beetles, and spends time with his wife's family, and his daughter.

I was, and am, fucking astonished. He sent me a picture of the family, and I sent him one of our little household. It was nice.

Of course the pace of the correspondence didn't stay fast and furious, but we did talk about the island a lot. It was occasionally infuriating because I would keep asking him things, and he wouldn't know the answers. Landers is one of those people who seems to have no curiosity about anything but his field. He was also hesitant to ask the locals much. His wife, to be honest, seemed to consider questions rude.

I applied for a visa, and I waited and waited and waited, and so did he, though he mentioned that if they asked him, he'd put in a word for me. I never expected to be able to visit. I didn't think I'd ever get a visa, and I didn't think I could afford it. Of course, I couldn't afford it, as it happens but that didn't actually stop me.

Landers and I have been friends, and intentional brothers for about five years, though our contact had diminished recently. Life is busy, and let's face it, he lives across the world from me. I never lost sight of the fact or the feeling that in some way there was this piece of me who lived in a place out of my childhood dreams. It made both Landers and the island seem so much more real.

And this is why I had to go to Sel Souris. And this is why I have another brother, and another niece for that matter, that I don't really mention much. Sel Souris and Landers have always been my secret emotional hiding spot, if that makes sense. My private place of happy.

It doesn't, I realize, explain why I've no pictures. So I'll sum it up quickly as the preface to the next part of the story, which I will keep adding to until I spill it all out. The reason I have no pictures is two-fold. Number one, the people who live there are very touchy about photos. They're not "EEK! You have taken my soul" touchy, but they don't like them. This includes Lander's wife, Mirat. Number two is best explained with my story of the trip to the tail of Sel Souris.

Tomorrow the travelogue/family drama begins.

Flight

The plane smells of cigar smoke. Nasty. It also smells of ouzo. It's cold, and the pilot gestures roughly at a pink and purple checked woolen blanket. The blanket is stained but it looks warm. My bag is tossed in the back. I squeeze into the co-pilot seat. This is awkward and weird. I am not a small man. The pilot sees that I am in, and takes a hit off a bottle right in front of me, and then, as an afterthought, offers it to me. I shake my head and smile. He shrugs and puts the bottle back in his pocket. My stomach rolls with fear. It is clear to both of us that he speaks not a word of English.

He starts the ignition and we begin taxi down the runway. He drives the plane in a wide circle and then heads straight down the strip which ends in a sharp drop to the sea. For a second we drop off the edge and then with another stomach toss gain altitude.

The pilot gives a laugh like an accordion with a hole in it, which tapers to a wheeze. He looks at me and smiles. I weakly smile back, or try to. Actually, god only knows what my face looks like.

If I understood the people at the airstrip the flight to Sel Souris is two hours. All I can see out the windscreen is black, and the winking red and white lights on the plane itself. If he spoke English, I'd ask him how he was navigating. I assume it's by instrument. I know nothing about airplanes, though this trip has taught me I prefer the experience of the small plane to the airliner. It's less warm, but less artificial and icky. It might be different in the daylight, I expect. I'm exhausted from sleeping in spurts across the trip, and even though I am positive the pilot is drunk I fall into a light sleep.

Beside me, the pilot sings softly under his breath. The song is completely not familiar, but the sound of of his voice is deeply comforting to me, and I feel safe even as the fumes from his bottle drift through the cockpit.

He nudges me gently, and gestures to the right. I look out the screen and I can see lights on the sea. I feel a twinge because it's too dark for me to see the shape of the island at night.

The landing is rough. He's had two more hours of drinking, and for a few seconds before the wheels touch the pavement I am sure we are going nose first into hell. Then the wheels squeak and the plane lurches. I throw up a little in my mouth, and he laughs a crazy drunken laugh. We taxi to a stop, and he grabs my bag and hands it to me. We shake hands formally and I thank him. The airport is a prefabricated tin building just at the end of the airstrip.

I walk in and am surprised to find the lights are out. I flip the switch and turn on the lights. It's a small room. On the counter is a small bell. Not the sort you'd typically see. It's a hand bell, small and silver. I pick it up and ring it.

"Hello," I say.

Another light comes on, and a man comes out. He's about sixty, grey and black hair, dark tanned skin, and pale eyes. He is wearing a robe in a shocking bright pink, and his pyjama bottoms are of a similar colour.

"Mr. States?" he says approaching the desk.

"Yes," I say, "I'm sorry to wake you up."

He waves his hand, to dismiss it.

"I was expecting. We spoke on the telephone. Passport please."

I hand him my passport and he examines it as cursorily as I have ever seen it done and stamps it.

"Welcome to Sel Souris." He reaches under the counter, and pulls out a small booklet held together by brass fasteners like one would see on an old duo-tang. It's about 3" by 5", and I open it up. It has my name on it, and the permissible duration of my stay. He nods, and reaches for it. I hand it over and he checks his watch, and alters the times to match 48 hours from the present time.

Jesus. I had no idea at all.

I take it back and thank him. Another man comes in the building. He is young and dressed in a dark blue shirt and matching trousers that look like linen. I have seen Indian men wearing outfits very similar, but I have no idea what they're called. I could tell you facts about Kryptonite that would wow you, but there are certainly a lot of practical things I don't know.

"Your hotel, mister?" he says to me.

"Oh god, please yes," I say, and he laughs. I don't think he understands the joke, but he can tell I'm making one.

"Your brother, the bug man, sent me."

I smile.

"Yes. He told me he would. Thanks."

I take my bag to the car, and he opens the door for me.

The trip to my hotel is like driving through an old movie. Even this early people are up and about on the streets, setting up their shops. They are walking cattle down the street. They are all dressed in bright and gaudy clothes, tending to pinks and purples. They stare at the cab with deep hostility. The driver notices that I am seeing the hostility.

"The car, Mister Ryan, is French. They do not like the French here. They mostly do not like me either. It is not you, it is this place," he explains, with the singing lilt of the Indian accent. "I am from Calcutta. This is a better place."

I nod.

"I bet. How long have you been here?"

"Ten years. This is a long time, but to them I am still a stranger. Even more than your bug man. I am too British for them. These are crazy people, here, but kind. I would be dead if they had not let me stay."

"If they hate you so much why did they let you stay?"

"I was just a child when I arrived. Your hotel, sir."

The car stops. I have more questions, but I need sleep, and it would seem weird to push. I thank him and pay him a ridiculous amount of money for a twenty minute drive, and a tip.

The hotel clerk speaks almost no English, and I speak no Basque, if that's what he speaks. And it might be, some here do.

We manage to get me checked in. I do have a reservation. He leads me up the hall to one of the five rooms this place has. To my shock, the room has an internet hookup. I log on, and send a few emails, and do a blog post.

Then I fall back onto the bed, still dressed, and fall asleep on what I will soon discover is a feather pillow. I will discover this by nearly dying of asthma. But in this moment, I sleep as deeply as death.

Asleep on Sel Souris. The strangest place on Earth. And what a long strange trip it's already been.

Now I am hungry, and onward I go to make a sandwich. Which is the most grounding experience in the world. And nice too, you know. Enjoy those moments, kids.

Back at work, and writing in bits and pieces.

I wake up choking and gasping, feeling faint. I look at the alarm clock and it's early morning. I've barely slept. I've slept in my clothes, with my glasses on. I am really very aware of not breathing well, and my face itches. I sit up, and my chest aches. I prod the pillow. Fuck. Feathers.

Ventolin, I think, please for fuck's sake let me have brought Ventolin. I don't want to die here in this place. I am terrified because it would be like me to head across the world and forget. I rifle through my pockets, and in my coat pocket I find it. I thank Ganesh for looking after beggars and fools. In a few minutes I feel vaguely ill and dizzy but I can breathe again, so it feels amazing. I look at the room for a few minutes.

It's small. There's no television, which is really odd from my small experience of hotel rooms and it is the first thing to jump out. The floors are a rich dark uncarpeted wood. The walls are a pale pink stucco. I need to shower. I look at the room, and it becomes clear to me there is no bathroom here. Okay. It must be shared for the floor. I grab my bag and I head into the hall. Across the hall is another room and, down the hall, there is the washroom.

I shower with cold water and the entire time the pipes give off hisses and clicks that are a little disconcerting but I do get clean. The soap is really strong and harsh and scented with something unfamiliar and musky. The itching from the feathers stops. A different kind of itching from the soap begins. I prefer it.

I head back to my room and look at my travel clock. I've slept about three and a half hours and paid about two hundred dollars for it. I have a theory that they only allow 48 hour visas here out of a misguided sense of morality. Any longer than that and the gouging would break you. Still, that's why they let you in. They need the money. I try not to think that these are American dollars and think of the exchange rate to Canadian dollars. Why make it worse?

I'm hungry. I head downstairs. The lobby smells of fresh smoke. It smells good to me. An old man is sitting on a wooden chair by the window. He is dressed in blue jeans and an Adidas t-shirt. He has dark plastic sunglasses and is singing in French. He stops the moment he hears me and looks afraid. He says something high and questioning in a language I don't know at all. He looks toward me, and I can tell he's blind.

"Hello," I say, quietly, remembering I'm breaking a law, "Bonjour?"

"Hello," he says. "He back in a few minutes."

I ask him in halting French where I can find something to eat. He either pretends not to understand, or my French is so bad that he really can't. Either one is plausible considering what these people think of the French. I excuse myself and I am about to leave when the proprietor returns. He turns to the old man and shouts at him gesturing wildly and the old man bows his head and heads into the back.

"You have a message, sir."

He hands me a slip of paper with a smooth satiny sheen and I read it. It's Landers' number and the instruction I'm to call him. I smile and I ask if there is a phone. He gestures at the wall and I dial him up.

"Hello," a girl answers.

"Hello," I say, "Is this Faiza?"

"Yes," she says in English that sounds accentless, "who is this?"

"I'm Ryan States," I say.

She squeals a little, and I hear her call for her father. She calls him Daddy.

There are a few moments of rustling and Landers comes to the phone.

I need to stop here, because I'm not yet ready to share that. The further I get along in this story, the more miserly I feel myself getting with details. So much happened in almost no time, and it was all so important to me.

Tomorrow I'll talk about meeting my niece and my sister-in-law and about actually putting my arms around all of them.

I'll skip the awful breakfast of hard black bread and goat butter and the rickshaw (or whatever it was) ride out to the southern end of Sel Souris, and I'll start from meeting my family for lunch and tea. I hope anyone is still reading after so many days of nothing. I just don't want to waste it.

Writing this makes me sad. More tomorrow.

Just returned from G's company Christmas party.

Much fun had by all. At this party, I was able to learn the answer to one question already brought up in these accounts.. The traditional Indian garment my cab driver wore is called a Kurta Pyjama. It's a traditional formal garment. Finding this out charms me a little more. It turns out that his wearing the Kurta to drive the cab would be like doing so in a suit.

The name of the driver, by the way, is Sanjit. (Hello Sanjit, I hear you're trapped on an island of strangers. Welcome to my blog.)

My Sel Souris travelogue continues.

My ass, ladies and gentlemen, is sore as I see the house. My carriers, and by god, I am not comfortable with that, announce to me in smatters of English that we are approaching the Bug Man's house. We've headed south out of the town of Sel Souris, and toward the peninsula. The town dwindles gradually into tacked together shacks with vegetable gardens. Pigs and chickens wander in the road, but the boys seem familiar with it, and it doesn't slow us down. After a surprisingly short while there's almost nobody. I've noticed that the faces have gotten darker the further we've traveled. The island has a strange admixture of peoples. Mostly out this far are North African Arabs, the descendants of people brought in by the French to work the salt.

The house is a bungalow, built recently, and it doesn't seem fit. As I understand it, he had it shipped in pre-fabricated pieces, and it was assembled from instructions. It's tucked in at the southern coast, not far from deposits of salt, and you can see the peninsula stretch out from the yard. The salt is hard on the grass, and I can see what tries to pass for a lawn. I also notice the preponderance of beetles.

Even though I expected this, I didn't realize. The ground is thick in places with the iridescent dark purple beetles, each of them the size of a large man's thumb. It's a strange mixture of eerie beauty and total revulsion. I can hear the clicking sounds as their carapaces slide over each other. The smell of salt is intense and I look at the whitewashed house and wonder how the siding holds up.

For some reason I have nothing to do but think this, and I pay my carriers another princely sum. I don't even know what to tip. I am nearly out of cash, and I'm concerned about getting a cash advance somewhere. For not the fifteenth time I wish I'd planned this better.

"Ryan?" says a tall blond man with curly hair and a deep tan. He is dressed in jeans and a beige silk shirt that an open neck and laces up. He is smiling, and his teeth seem very white.

I walk quickly over to him, and as I get closer, I feel myself smiling, and I look at his face. Thin, angular, but in the curve of his lips and especially in the eyes, I see it, and it's real.

"Hi," I say, and it's all I can say, my eyes feeling a little hot and moist to actually be here.

"It's good to meet you," he says, and we stand there, trying to decide if we should hug, or shake hands or what exactly. The strangeness of it is overwhelming. Before we come to a conclusion on that I am taken at the waist in two small dark arms and a face slams into my chest, hugging me. I give a little oof.

Faiza squeezes me, and says a number of things directly to my stomach that I don't understand at all. I hug her back.

"Hello there."

"Hi!" she looks up at me, and smiles. Her eyes are a big deep dark brown. Her face is round and young, and her hair, my god, is gorgeous. Her mother's dark hair and her father's blond mixing into a kind of rippled creme caramel that is hers alone, I think. She is going to be a very pretty woman in a few years, and she's not shy.

"Hi Faiza."

Landers' wife comes out. She is shorter than me, but not by much. She is dressed in a white linen dress. Her dark hair is very long, and naturally kinky and pulled back with a leather thong. She smiles politely and comes to greet me.

"You must be Mirat," I say.

"Welcome," she says, and kisses both my cheeks, embracing me. There is no warmth or enthusiasm in it. She is being polite. I accept it, and return the kisses briskly. She knows that I am bisexual, and to her that makes me questionable. It's already bad enough that I am from North America, but to be that and also a queer is, I think, a little much for her religion. She is not showing hostility and is being quite graceful. I let it go.

She steps back and puts an arm around Landers' waist, and I can see in the way their eyes meet that theirs is a pretty intense thing. Love, marriage, a nice kid. It's not what I want, but I'm glad for him.

Faiza is chattering at me, and is a little clingy. It's cute. She seems young for her age. Thirteen is a very tough age, you want all the teenaged treatment, but sometimes you just want to be held and cuddled and picked up and treated like a kid. She's so excited that she keeps hopping. We talk about Canada, as we go inside, and I dig in my bag and I give her a little book I picked up at the airport, pictures of Canada. She starts to flip through it.

Landers and Mirat hold hands as we go up the lane, and I'm ushered into the living room. The furniture is wicker, and I don't want to trash the place so I opt to sit on the floor. I insist on it, despite their protestations. I explain that when a man gets to my size there's only so much that hospitality is expected to afford. I like sitting on the floor. Mirat excuses herself to make tea.

Faiza and I keep talking. Landers is amused, and our eyes meet, smiling. I'm not surprised he's comfortable with not talking. It turns out that Faiza is home schooling, and taking some classes over the internet. They have a satellite connection. I think to myself that must cost a small fortune, but it turns out that USC is paying for it. Landers pipes up with that, and Faiza rolls her eyes at being interrupted. We both laugh.

She's probably a great kid, but it's clear she sees very few strangers, and she's way over-enthusiastic in a cute way but one which is gonna tire us both out. I don't actually mind. It's not all that often I'm greeted with this much enthusiasm.

Her mother comes in a few minutes later, with a tray. A teapot and 3 cups, and some metal canisters.

"Faiza," Mirat says, "go outside and read for ten minutes and let your uncle breathe."

Reluctantly Faiza looks at her mother. She pleads in what I am pretty sure is Arabic, and her mother replies with a sharp single syllable. Faiza looks to her father who grins and points his thumb at the door.

"Outside, daughter of daughters."

Faiza sticks her tongue out at him and then recovers her dignity to stalk off.

"I'm sorry," Landers says. "She's been like this since yesterday."

"I so very much totally do not mind.

"Would you like tea?" Mirat offers.

"Thank you, yes."

"How was the hotel?" he asks me, as Mirat pours the straw coloured tea into our mugs.

"I should have checked the pillows," I said. "I'm allergic to feathers. I wasn't thinking."

Mirat smirks a little, her intent opaque.

"Yeah," he says, "You get used to that. My first year here I had to keep reminding myself about things like that."

"Do you like your tea sweet?" Mirat asks me.

"That depends on the type of tea. How do you drink it?" She looks at Landers and he smiles. He smiles easily.

"It's an acquired taste," he says.

I'm intrigued and I sit back.

"How do you drink it?"

Mirat takes her cup and takes a tiny dollop of cream in it, and she stirs it until the milk is blended in. Then she opens one of the metal canisters and takes in her pinched thumb and forefinger a little pinch of purple and pink powder. She sprinkles it atop the tea like glitter, and Landers does the same.

"Is that what I think it is?"

Mirat sips her tea, and smiles.

"When God gives you beetles in such abundance, you find uses in abundance."

I nod, and I take a small pinch and sprinkle it atop the tea. It looks strange. The tea is jasmine, I think, but now there is another odor. I take the metal canister of ground beetle and inhale above it. It smells of wood chips and chocolate and fruit, and yet not really any of those things. Once again I realize I am not in Canada, and that things are different here.

I am in Sel Souris, but actually being here makes it impossible to see it as just the legend. It's a place, and the people are just people. This, the beetles in my tea, pulls me back and out of the experience. I sip the tea and my sinuses burn with a feeling like menthol lozenges.

"Slowly," Mirat says, "It will surprise you."

It has. The look on my face must let that show.

Landers laughs again, this time at the expression on my face, and as I set the cup down, he comes over, and kneels beside me on the floor and wraps his arms around me in a hug.

"I'm already so glad you came, man."

Tears spring uninvited down my cheeks, and into my beard, and I hold onto him. There's a strange sense of relief and comfort in this. When you meet someone at a distance, you never know how it will be in person, and you worry that the distance is all that made you friends, that face to face, you'll be strangers again, shy like three year old kids.

I weep like one, in big sobs, like I've been holding it in for a dozen years, and didn't know it. Maybe it's the vibe of this whole insane trip coming clear in this moment. Mirat rolls her eyes and sips her tea. Landers has told me she dislikes emotional displays.

In this moment, I don't care.

"I have so much to show you," he says.

He squeezes me once more and then pulls back. I wipe my face, laughing a little, embarrassed.

"Men," Mirat says, "Warriors and hunters, every one."

I laugh harder and Landers reaches over to tickle her, and she slaps his hand away playfully.

I sip my tea, and I'm ready for it now. I wonder what the hell is in this, and if it can possibly be good for me. It is tasty though, in its way, and I've never had anything like it before.

We sip tea and make small talk. The beetles crawl all over the house, and my hosts don't seem to mind or notice. I try not to either. The people of Sel Souris have a strong feeling of kinship to these beetles, and it's taboo to deter them. It's not taboo to eat them, however, or to make dye of them. They have their freedom, it seems, until they have their use.

Landers is here now because he got Mirat pregnant. It's clear that he doesn't regret that. He explained this to me a while ago. He came for the beetles. He's the expert on them. He's the only expert. A lot of beetles have their own expert. There are a

LOT of different species of beetles. He and I have discussed this. He is very passionate on the topic. He says there are so many beetles because they are perfect. I get his point.

You can get used to the strangest things.

We finish our tea, and I am aware that the tea has left me with a mild buzz. I make a mental note of the stimulant of choice on Sel Souris. It is no mystery to me now as to what it is I have seen some people chewing here. I thought it might be tobacco or betel nuts. Wrong.

Landers looks good, strong, though I notice his head does sometimes have a mild wobble to it. It makes my stomach hurt a little. He did not, I have to admit, get ALL the good genes.

We talk for awhile about my trip and about his work. There is no electricity right now out here. They have electricity at scheduled hours of the day. Later I will be able to post from his computer, and I'm pleasantly surprised.

He offers to show me around the island, and I smile.

"Can we start with the peninsula?" I ask, grinning. He knows the peninsula is half of why I'm here.

"No," he says. "It's better at night. And there's the tradition."

He is very serious as he says this, but not heavy. I don't know if he has heavy in him.

"Tradition," Mirat says, and there is no frivolity about her. "When family comes, or when a person is chosen to stay..."

"Decides to stay," Landers says, correcting her English mildly. She looks at him and nods impatiently, rolling her eyes.

"Yes, yes, decides to stay. When a person decides to stay, it is important they understand this place, and what has happened here so that it never happens ever again."

I nod solemnly. The people on this island have suffered deep wounds that have gone on to the subsequent generations. I know some already, but I know there is more, as I have always known, far more than the annals of accepted history would have us know.

My heart is pounding in my chest. For an instant, I'm seven and standing at the brink of total enlightenment. I am in the strangest, and maybe the saddest, place in the world.

"I'll tell you the whole thing," Landers says. "You can try tell the world if you like."

"They won't listen," Mirat says.

He turns to her.

"Well, he can try."

She nods.

"You can try."

I swallow hard. I'm not sure I'm ready for this. I came halfway around the world for it. I expect I'll get ready.

Tomorrow, I'll try tell the world about what happened in Sel Souris. They might listen. Like Mirat, I doubt it. She knows what she's talking about.

Under the weather

I'm at home today, my bronchitis is back, this time with the cough. Sorry for the lateness of the post. Thought I'd better write it up now. I worry that the details will start to go on me. They do that so quickly, and I need to get it all down.

Mirat pulls Faiza to her schoolwork, and Landers and I get into his battered green Toyota. It is all rusted out, which is not surprising considering the salt. It seems to run okay. He is a nervous driver, he leans forward as he drives. We take the same road back toward town that I took coming out. I don't know if I should talk, partly because of the whole somber tone of the trip, but also because he is so very focused on driving. I notice that it seems to take more time by car than it did by rickshaw (or, again, whatever you call it).

He takes a left, and squints at direct sunlight.

"This road seems longer going back than it did coming up," I offer.

"It does that. Whole place is like that. You should try living here."

He smiles without looking at me, eyes on the road.

Until this moment it never occurred to me that was even possible. I supposed it might be. Not that I'd find work, and frankly not that I'd want to. Increasingly I am aware that the island is a nice place to visit, but that it's no place I could live.

He brakes suddenly inhaling sharply. He looks at me.

"Keep quiet," he says.

I don't dream of doing anything else.

The reason I don't dream of it is that two teen boys with olive skin have approached the road at either side with terrifying rifles nearly as tall as they are.

They don't point the rifles at us. They hardly need to. My heart is beating in my throat. The soldiers look at me but don't speak to me. They speak to Landers.

He turns to me, "They need to see your visa. Not your passport. Don't show your passport."

I swallow trying to stay calm. What I know is this: My visa is folded inside my passport which is in my breast pocket.

I reach for my breast pocket, and they shift the guns. I fumble in my pocket, and I smile weakly as I try to pull my visa out of the passport by a fingernail's edge. I feel it pull free, and I am deeply and profoundly grateful as I hand it to Landers who hands it to them.

The boys glance at it and they make small talk with Landers for a few minutes and then they hand the visa back. I am wondering what my friends and family would think if I'd been shot just now, or had my passport stolen. Of course, I then realize I've not even told my family. Jesus. I don't even know how to tell my family. I've not even told my Mom I've been in touch with Landers. I close my eyes and breathe, and the boys head back to wherever they were.

"Holy fuck." I breathe loudly, even for me.

"Welcome to Sel Souris," he says. "Friendliest place on earth."

"I've never seen a gun like those. Not in real life."

"AK-47. Standard issue for the Sel Souris militia."

"Wow. How do you deal with that all the time?"

Landers shrugs, still leans forward to it.

"You get used to the strangest things," he says.

My stomach flips, and I don't know why.

"Wow."

"It wasn't as bad as you might think. The scrawny one who thinks he has a moustache is Mirat's brother. We were in no danger of being shot. But he might have stolen your passport."

"I am no good at traveling. I should have thought about that myself. Stupid."

He laughs. I like the sound of his laugh. I'm getting accustomed to it.

"Y'know, your visa would have been approved any old time. It's crazy you came here like this. I can't believe it. If I was one of your friends I don't know if I'd be speaking to you right now. I mean, I'm glad and all but it seems a bit, well, pardon me for saying this, but it seems a bit crazy."

"Yeah. That's sort of been occupying my mind ever since I left."

"I bet."

"I just worried that, and I know this will sound crazy too, that, if I didn't go right fucking now, something or someone would find a way to make me not do this."

He nods.

"Yeah. That sounds familiar."

"Gayleen always tells people that my central problem is an excess of whimsy."

"Yin and Yang."

"Hm?"

"I don't have enough whimsy. I never have. I lived a very button down life until I moved here. And, well, this place," he pauses, inclining his head slightly, "is not really good for whimsy."

We go past a cluster of over hanging trees and come to a flat area without grass. The soil is a hard baked brown. Little scraps of green are trying to scrabble their way to life ineffectually. The area extends from the road to the coast. It's maybe a couple of miles to the coast from here, and it's wide too. There's a tall wooden post and some benches and plaques up the way what I estimate to be the equivalent of a four or five blocks in. He stops the car, and takes a breath.

"We walk it from here," he says. He rifles behind him on the seat and he offers me a pair of rubber boots, and a pair of rubber gloves. I take them.

I put them on, awkwardly with the door open. Landers puts his own on. He doesn't lock the door to his car. For some reason that strikes me odd. What doesn't?

What I notice, almost immediately is that the grass stops suddenly, giving way to sun-baked soil. Where the grass stops, the beetles stop.

There are no beetles on this field, and no people or animals. It is then I realize exactly where I am. I swallow hard.

"This is Nowhere," he says. "Follow me. Don't touch anything."

I follow him. To nowhere, apparently.

We walk up towards the post, and I can hear every footstep. The boots are too small, and it's kind of painful. We don't talk.

When we get to the post, I see a block of plastic mounted on it. In this block are what look like two eyeballs staring toward the coast, optic nerves suspended in Lucite and ragged.

There is a hand lettered sign on dark wood. "I can't read this," I say to him.

"It says, 'England sees now,'" he says.

I look to him, and he nods.

"Jesus."

"Yeah. His family is still trying to get them back. For some damned reason. It will never happen. These people would take a direct nuclear attack over surrendering those eyes."

I shake my head.

"Why would anyone do that?"

"Well, some people are funny about dead bodies, you know, like you can't lay them to rest properly without every last bit. Never mind the flakes of skin..."

"No," I say. "I mean, why would they do THAT with his eyes."

He blinks, looking at me.

"Yeah," he says eventually, "I guess that would seem weird to you."

Which tears it for me in a moment. I don't want this fucking spectacle to ever seem less strange to me than it does right now, or less horrible. This island is fucking crazy.

He sees the expression on my face.

"I know," he says. "Believe me. I have a daughter here. If I could talk Mirat into leaving, we would, beetles or not. It's not an option. So I've made peace with it."

"I get that, and I understand and all that but—Landers, man, how did you not go crazy getting used to this?"

He smiles.

"Lots and lots of tea."

And I'll stop there for now because if I don't, this entry will be far, far too long. More tomorrow, if all goes well.

Seam and Interface

Hi guys, sorry for the lateness of this part. I wrestled with posting the whole conversation in one lump and then I decided I just couldn't do it. I wrestled with just skipping this part, actually. Because this is where a strange story becomes balls up crazy. And more than a little sad.

"How dangerous is this place?" I ask.

"Pretty dangerous if you stayed here for hours."

"Well," I said, "We won't do that then."

"Heh. Yeah."

I already know what happened here more or less. In 1890, the French governor allowed the testing of an early experimental gas weapon on the eastern coast of the island. No care was taken to warn the local inhabitants, and a stiff wind carried the gas into the main settlement. In four hours half of the people of Sel Souris died. Not one of them was a representative of a European nation. The French had their people evacuated for the sake of safety and, out of courtesy, also warned the handful of English and Spanish merchants in harbor. A large section of the island was considered uninhabitable, and the governor did not return.

The locals seized control of the weapons, and what there was of an economy, and set in place laws that have remained more or less unchanged to this day. The massacre at Sel Souris did not make the news. At all. For years. Europe quietly turned their back on Sel Souris and waited for the island to just go away.

The island was rediscovered in the late 1950s by the American fringe press and they held Sel Souris up as a classic example of the horrors of colonialism. For about 8 years they covered the island furiously, and tourist traffic from the States brought money to the island. Then people stopped talking about the incident. The detail got fuzzier. It became the province of cranks and then it sunk like a rock until only two pretty small groups even noted it. Entomologists, on account of the beetle, and students of the weird and unexplained.

And so it goes.

"So," he said. "How much do you know already?"

"Not much," I said, "just a gas test that turned into a tiny little Bhopal."

"Okay."

"I'm assuming it was an early phosgene? I don't know much about it."

He nodded.

"No. It was biological."

"Oh."

"And the French didn't bring it here to test. It's worse than that."

"How the fuck is it worse?"

"They made it here. Right about where we're standing, and they used it on purpose to kill off the last original inhabitants of Sel Souris."

I say nothing for a few seconds.

"Can we finish this talk in the car? I really don't want to stand here anymore."

He looks me in the eyes.

"The peninsula is nothing to this place. Where you're standing is the same place that aliens lived for over sixty years."

I laugh.

"Shut up," I say, starting back to the car laughing.

He doesn't move.

"And this is where we killed them. All of them."

I've heard all the craziest of crazy stories about this place. I've never known what was speculation, and I've never known what was plain made up, or what was exaggeration. I've read theories and accounts, always vague and unsupported, and it was okay because in my gut this place was as remote and theoretical as Alpha Centauri.

Now I am standing in the middle of what is unmistakably a poisoned place, and this man who is my half brother is saying out loud things that were considered too crazy for the cranks to do more than laugh off as superstition. And he means it. I stop walking, but don't turn around.

"It's not folklore, and it's not superstition. It's history, man. It's the history that nobody wants to know. It's the most shameful thing we've ever done in our stupid and bloody history. I absolutely know why nobody wants to believe it. I wish I didn't have to."

"It's crazy," I say, turning around. "Are you hazing me?"

He shakes his head.

"It's not funny."

"No," I say, "It's not."

"You told me in one of your letters that you were like Fox Mulder. You've spent your whole life wanting to believe."

"Not in this!"

"Too bad," he says quietly, "because this is how it is."

The cruelty of this moment is all wrapped in the subversion of my fondest desire into my biggest fear. My stomach hurts. You know how people feel about pets? It's a kind of wonder that's based in how we can be so different, so limited in our ability to communicate with each other, and yet belong to each other so completely. It's the embodiment of the fact that different doesn't have to be scary, that it doesn't have to divide us. Our differentness is what makes us love each other.

I have always harboured a fantasy that it would be the same with aliens from another planet. That we would instinctively belong, and that it would be a kind of love. I wanted to believe, I still, in this moment, do believe that in the vast gulf of space if we find each other we will crave each other like men and dogs do. Maybe more so, because we would really understand how huge and empty the universe is, and how precious we are to each other.

I don't want to hear this story because, if it's true, we don't belong. We don't deserve it. I feel my eyes getting hot, and I am frustrated with myself, because I hate crying, even though I know it's stupid, and because this is the second time I've cried today.

"Fuck," I say.

Landers walks over to me.

"Fucking cry, man. It's sad. This place is sad. It's beautiful because it's sad, and it's strange because it's sad."

"Tell me."

"Nobody knows the whole story, because it started before we got here. In 1757, it landed, whatever it was. Whether it fell from outer space or not we have no idea. We have no idea where it came from, or who they were. The early accounts talk about the beetles swarming on the bare earth. Which makes no sense. Beetles don't come from nowhere. They don't, mostly, swim, and they rarely do something like a migratory swarm. There wasn't time. If the island had just been here and nobody noticed, there'd have been plants, other animals. There wasn't. It's very clear. Bare earth and beetles."

"Yeah," I say, starting to walk.

"Once they introduced plants to the island they took root and spread fast. The beetles still remained the dominant animal on the island.

The first colony didn't make it. They died of a plague. The reports are hazy. So the island was left to beetles and plants. In the interim, something happened. I don't know exactly what it was. Scientifically, I don't have an explanation. I don't even really have a…folkloric explanation."

There's a tone in the way he says it, and I can tell he doesn't feel comfortable with this part of the story.

"People felt the urge to come here. I've heard the same story from family after family, and they all talk about it the same way. They felt a call to leave the places they didn't belong. The Basque, the Catalonians, the Roma. They found the island and went there because it felt like their brothers calling them home. And when they got here, they were not alone. And they didn't die."

He takes a deep sigh.

"Fuck," Landers says. "This story sounds crazier every time I tell it."

I look at him, and I try to smile.

"I'm pretty sure you're not wrong about that."

My eyes study him, looking for signs of a put on. I'm not seeing any. On the other hand, I know that I have a talent for saying the craziest things, without a trace of put on. He's my brother, so who knows?

"Okay," he says. "Time out for a minute. We're going to head into town, and I'm going to show you a corpse."

"Of an alien."

"I believe so. But you won't see me writing a paper about it anytime soon."

"I would probably re-blog that," I say wryly.

"Good luck with that," he says, smiling back at me. For a moment the tension and the weirdness is gone. I really like him. I really do. Even if he's batshit crazy, which I have begun to wonder about, I really like him.

He sees me looking at him, and he pats my back.

"Me too, bud. Me too."

More to come, of course. Talk to you tomorrow.

A Pain In My Head, Where The Dreams Hammer Home

Welcome back to The Rook's Nest, where fat men ramble about their travels.

In the car we head back to the townsite. Some people wave at Landers as he drives hunched over the wheel like a ninety year old woman. He waves back. My stomach flips.

He and I make small talk, neither of us referencing the deep weirdness of the day's events so far. The colours of everything are, and I have to use this word, unspeakably vivid. A handful of beetles roll and twist on the seat between us, and it's like I see invisible lines of force connecting the shiny exoskeletons and the paint on the walls of the buildings, the colours on the shirts and shifts and trousers of the locals. The beetles are everywhere, and into everything and every beautiful thing here that is not green. The noise of mandibles clicking like morse code of some urgent message the entire island is trying to remember.

I am suddenly aware that I am in the headspace where I practice and perceive magic most acutely. I don't know if it's stress or being overwhelmed with the exotic or sleep deprivation or the beetle tea, but I am in an altered state.

Laird Ryan States

Sel Souris is an altered state, it occurs to me, awash in bright purple dreams that don't belong here. This place has been changed and re-written. I feel my blood moving in my skin, and for what is only a second, I hear the call. I want Landers to stop this car and let me out. I want to lie on bare loam, and burrow deep into the cool earth and press myself to the beating heart underneath, to feel the repeated pressing heat of blood as it pushes though and through and through.

"In my life," Vin says to me, 16 years ago, quoting Wuthering Heights, "I have dreamt such dreams that have gone through and through me like water through wine, and altered forever the colour of my mind."

"Vin?" I say out loud, and I see him at the side of the road, his three-lobed skull filled with eyes, each tuned to a different spectrum of electromagnetism.

Landers shoves me gently, "Stay with me, man. Don't drift."

I shake my head, and take my glasses off, so I can rub my eyes with the heel of my hand.

"Sorry," I say, "I'm really tired."

"Yeah. Well, that's probably true, but you'd be amazed how many people who hear these stories suddenly feel the need to go to sleep."

"I want to stay here," I say to him.

"No. You don't. You're just saying that because you've slept like five hours in two days, and you're really emotional and stoned on the tea."

I shake my head. "Okay."

I don't see any reason to argue with him. I think that when you're traveling, you may as well listen to your guides. They probably know what they're talking about.

He stops the car outside a small two story stucco building. The front of it has a deep crack from which the beetles crawl and and clack. Landers leads me inside the door, and we walk up the long narrow staircase to the area upstairs. In this room is a deep freeze and a table with another computer on it, and there are jars of dead beetles on shelves filled with papers and books.

"This is my office," Landers says. "Such as it is."

"Nice?" I say, and he laughs.

"Okay," he says, clearing a space on a table. He goes to the deep freeze and opens it. He removes a ziploc bag from the freezer, and lays it on the table before he carefully opens it and using a plastic tong, pulls out something that is wrapped up in tissue paper. He carefully peels the tissue paper back to reveal the contents within. I gasp, actually fucking gasp, at what I see. My head goes swimmy and I think I might hurl right here on top of this...this fucking miracle, and so I turn away. He puts a hand on my shoulder, and mumbles something that sounds concerned and supportive.

I turn back around. I have to look again. The creature in the paper looks as though it was pickled at one time, and is now nearly freeze dried. I see the fine bones of its ribs under thin yellow parchment skin. The ribs look like a honeycomb, and my eyes feel drawn there to this feature, not wanting to look up higher.

I do. The creature's head is the size of a quarter, shaped like the head of a person. The eyes are faceted and iridescent. There is no nose, and at first, it seems to me, no mouth. I look closer and see I'm right. There is no mouth. A tiny neck connects the head to the torso. The arms are thin and spidery and covered in fine hairs, like the hairs on a dandelion stem, even after the freezer. There are no genitals, just thin little legs about the same length as the arms. Both the legs and arms end in perfect little hands with four tiny fingers and a thumb.

The creature is about as tall as a can of soda, but so slight.

Landers gently lifts the body and turns it over so I can see the tiny folded wings that form a pale translucent violet carapace on its back.

"Oh my god."

"I know."

He wraps the little thing back in tissue paper, and seals the bag, and puts it back in the freezer. He sits down, and I'm still staring at the place on the table where it laid.

There is, in my mind, no doubt that was once a living creature. I am a little ashamed of that. I always want to try and stay objective. I don't want to be a rube falling for the Fiji mermaid. I don't. If it isn't real, then believing in it isn't noble. It's stupid. I want it to be true. I don't want this to be true.

"Life was hard for the people who heeded the call, and they soon learned that they needed to stick together if they hoped to make it. Even the Roma set aside the concept of the outsider, and the people here clenched together like a fist to hold fast. The beetles were everywhere, and the people got used to them quickly."

I turn to watch him.

"About a year after they arrived, people began to see fairies. It was a joke at first, but as the years went on it became less of a joke. It also became more and more obvious that they weren't any fairies they'd heard of in the old country. They didn't fly, for one thing. They walked like people, and would sometimes stand still for an hour or two with their wings spread like little statues. Eventually they stopped talking of them as fairies altogether, and as just a part of life. There they were, after all."

I sit down, and I feel like I should say something, ask something, but I am now in so far over my head all I can do is listen.

"They didn't talk. They didn't use sign language, even with themselves, though people tried it with them. The fairies stuck mostly to the part of the island we were at this morning, where they lived in a series of mounds like termites build. People who went that far over to their part of the island, often came back feeling light headed and disoriented. Sometimes people fainted, and the fairies would carry them back to the road, and wait until the person came to before they departed. Sometimes, the fairies would bring woven cloth to the outside of the townsite and go home. The people of the town would leave cheese and wine by the road near the fairy mounds."

I look at my lap, very thirsty.

"So, even though there was no real communication, there was accommodation and trade of a kind. The people of the island had a sense that the fairies and the beetles had some relationship, but nobody really grasped it, and nobody felt they should look into it. The people here learned by observation that the crushed carapaces of the beetles were what the fairies used to dye the cloth, and it was also from the fairies that the people learned to add beetle to their tea."

I look up at him, and I speak for the first time since seeing the creature.

"Which, I'm guessing, changed everything?"

"Oh yeah. And so this place became a tight little community. Humans and fairies and the beetles living and working together for a couple of generations until nobody knew it had ever been different.

"When the French installed a governor, the whole island went into a spin. The governor and his men didn't care for the beetles, and that turned into a virtual uprising a half a dozen times. The townsfolk managed to keep the French away from the fairy mounds, claiming it as a sacred site. The Arabs brought in as virtual slave labour to work the salt heard stories from the townsfolk also conscripted, and assumed them to be earth elementals of some kind which fascinated most of them. Within ten years, the fairy mounds had diminished to a series of mostly unobtrusive lumps covered with short grass. The fairies were still seen, but not very often, and the locals assumed that they were moving on somehow.

"In 1885 things went to hell. A new governor was appointed who had no interest in humouring the pagan nonsense of the local savages and who felt it was a waste of beach front property. He had a warship summoned, and soldiers took the fairy village by storm, shooting any number of the townsfolk in the process. The remains of the village were pretty strange, and the governor found himself at the center of a lot of attention. The French government sent scientists to study. By 1887, the commotion was over, and the island got really quiet. The governor stopped weekly addresses to the town, and the fairy village was considered off-limits to anyone not a representative of the crown."

"Oh god," I say, getting it.

"Nobody really knows what happened out there. I've looked and if there are records of this with the French government, they're buried deep. I can tell you what I think happened."

"Okay," I say to him.

"I think the air was different there. I think the whole place was different. The fairies kept it different so that it would be more like home. When the French realized this, they thought they were looking at an invasion. Aliens from another world, coming to Earth and trying to change it. Hell, I don't actually think they were totally wrong about that. I think they spent several years examining what these creatures needed in a planet, and from that they made a good honest guess as to what would kill them. Then they did it."

We sit in silence for a few minutes.

"And so it goes," I say.

"Hi ho," he says, looking miserable.

"And the earth there is still that fucked up, after almost 120 years that nothing grows there? That the beetles won't even crawl there."

"Oh no. That wasn't the flesh eating gas," Landers says. "That shit all died within a couple of days."

"Then what?"

"That happened three hours later, when the island itself died."

I nod my head like I'm getting it, but it's more of a gesture of hopeless loss.

"There was a flash that turned night into day. The people saw French ships crumple like paper and vanish into nothing. They saw huge shadows and shapes moved in the night sky, and the island shook and strained and whined against the ocean and then it was dark and still, and the air was filled with smoke from the fairy village. There were a couple of fairies alive in the town, shaking and acting confused and disoriented after the gas, and at the moment the island went dark, they calmly laid down and died.

"And that is the story of mankind's first encounter with alien intelligence. It happened. It happened right here, and nobody will ever believe it. Nobody will ever admit to it. The French would have to admit what they did, and the rest of Europe would have to admit complicity.

"The people who live here, live on a corpse, desperate and angry and crazy that their whole life has been reduced from glory to a t-shirt slogan."

I shake my head. "T-shirt slogan?"

"My ancestors achieved symbiosis and peace with something strange and beautiful, and all I've got are these lousy beetles."

I laugh a strangled little laugh.

"Oh my god," I say. "My God."

"And so this is the story we tell our familes, that we tell people who have come here to live. The beetles sort of teach the rest in time. Which is hard to explain, but..."

"I get it a little already."

He nods.

"Let's go to the peninsula. It's what you came for."

I look him in the eyes.

"It's not all I came for. Can we just go home and see your wife and my niece? I...I need some time with you that isn't all tied up in this...stuff. I'll go crazy if I don't. I miss you already, and I haven't left the island yet. Isn't that stupid?"

"No, it isn't."

"I'll see the peninsula later. Like you said, it's better at night."

He nods, and we leave. He doesn't lock the door. As we leave people see the looks on our faces, and they look up to the office and look away. Nobody says anything.

I am a wreck, and I'm teary eyed, and life is so fucking beautiful and strange and sad, and one day it stops. I drink in the smells of this place as we drive home to where my family lives.

The roads are lined with the dead, hands linked, fairies on their shoulders waving goodbye to the living and green and the purple.

Tomorrow I visit the peninsula, and I wave goodbye to Sel Souris.

See you then.

We Tie Threads To Remember and Sever Knots With Swords

We drive back to the house in comfortable silence. I look out the window and try to take it in, the people, the scraggly grass, the ramshackle buildings, and the animals. There are pigs and goats and these small cattle everywhere. The livestock looks similar, but not exactly the same as back home though I can't place why.

The smell of the place is confusing, like durian fruit. It's such a combination of foul odours and deep green nature smell that my brain keeps trying to shut down. As we get closer to home I can see huge freighters off in the distance, ship smoke on the horizon, like the Pink Floyd song.

I am not comfortably numb. I am exhausted with sensation and knowledge and story and the smell of my brother not three feet from me. Another brother, and so strange to me. So much older than me in the way he acts, considering he's two years younger. I wonder if having a kid would age me like that. One more argument against.

He's driving hunched over and he's worried that I have taken the story badly, that I think he's crazy. I don't. I don't know what to believe, if to believe, or how much to believe. I know that if I lived here, if I chewed the beetles regularly I'd believe it all soon. I know what I saw in the freezer. I just don't have any idea what it was. I know that nobody will believe in it, and that is the way the world protects the strange from itself.

Jackie Gleason, the great one, used to tell people about the fact that aliens were real. When he was touring the Air Force bases, one of his fans, knowing he was interested in UFOs showed him the bodies of four aliens recovered from a crashed saucer. Gleason told this story to a lot of people.

Who better to tell than a comedian?

Every comedian I meet seems a little more serious and a little more broken than the one before. It's not that people don't believe comedians because they tell jokes. Comedians tell jokes because nobody believes them about anything. So what's left?

Jokes are what's left of us when sorrow washes our lives away.

Cue the drumroll.

We pull up out front of the house. When we get out I smell the sea, and from within the house, I smell something meaty and rich and my mouth fills with saliva like in a cartoon.

"Yikes," I say. "If that's supper, I hope I'm invited."

"It's goat," he says back, "so you may want to reconsider."

"Nope. I'll eat anybody once."

"Okay," he says. "A fine attitude."

I smile.

"Thank you, Landers."

He shrugs.

"I promise that when you come to Alberta, I will show you a bigfoot corpse. I promise. Could I do any less?"

He punches me in the shoulder without turning, right where G always gets me.

I laugh like crazy, and the front door opens and Faiza comes out and takes us each by the arm ushering us inside.

The dinner, the talk, the night of board games and the time I spent with my new relatives are not part of this story. I respect Landers and Mirat and their desire for some privacy. Frankly, there's no capturing it. It's not of much interest to anyone else. It was a night of board games with your family. You've done that. It was just like that. For a span of hours I set aside what I'd seen and heard. I surrounded myself with these people. It was lovely, and it was bittersweet and heavy with anticipatory grief.

It was almost certainly the only night I'd spend with them. All of us aware that this was a one time trip. And web-conferencing is no substitute.

Landers and Mirat had to practically lock Faiza in her room for bedtime. Then the grownups talked into the night, and Mirat excused herself to go to bed.

Landers and I were left alone and we discussed old science fiction books, and the radio play Gayleen and I were working on. He was amused that our lead actor is an entomologist.

"Entomologists," he said, "they get into everything."

Landers was sort of lightly toasted by three a.m., when we walked out the back, and up the peninsula. The sand gradually wore out to a black volcanic looking rock. It narrowed eventually to the extent that we walked single file. The house was a faded bright spot against the clinging coastal fog. A sweeping beam of light cut a shaft through the night spnning away in regular intervals, a lighthouse somewhere.

We stood quietly and I looked at the water, feeling the sense of motion you get, standing still, but surrounded by motion. As my eyes adjusted I realized the water surrounding the stone was glowing a pale purple that pulsed lightly. The light shone on my skin. I saw the mole on my wrist, and in this light it was there one second, and then not there and then back. I shook my head and blinked. I turned around to look at Landers.

His form seemed to shimmer in the light and the fog, and he seemed like a ghost. I stepped closer.

"Wow. This is strange. Am I just really tired, or is it always like this?"

"Always like what?"

"This light. It makes everything seem so unreal."

"It's always like that. Let's go back in."

It's the first time he's ever sounded impatient or unhappy.

"Okay," I say, trying to sound concerned, which is true, instead of disappointed, which is also true.

He turns and starts to walk back to the shore. The fog is thickening around us, and from time to time I lose sight of him. The purple light strobes from the water at the edge of my sight. I feel myself heading to shore, but my mind is in the water, diving to the base of the island. I hear the clicking of beetles and I realize they were waiting on the shore for us.

Landers is standing on the beach staring out at the water.

"That's all that's left of her," he says.

"What do you think it is?"

"I don't know. I think it's what's left of the engine. If this thing flew faster than light to get here, it had to be able to change all the rules somehow, and I think you'll agree the rules feel different out there."

"Yuh-huh."

We stand and listen to the waves lapping.

"Landers?" I say.

"Yeah?"

"Look, I'm a magician, and I can't just leave things at this. I need to go out there. Where the rules are different. If I don't I'll never sleep right again. I have to try to reach it. If it's there to be reached."

He nods.

"Go hard, man," he says, "never let it be said that I stood in the way of fate."

"Man," I say, "you stood in the way of fate."

He looks at me, raises an eyebrow.

"I don't like rules, square," I say, flipping up the collar of my imaginary leather jacket.

He wipes his eye with the heel of his hand and laughs.

"Jesus, man," he says, "I wish you were real."

"Me too," I say, and I wrap my arms around him. I kiss his neck where it meets his shoulder. He needs a shave. He smells of beetles and English Leather. We hold each other for a few minutes, and when I let him go, his sweet face fades and blows away on the stiff fog. In less time than it takes me to wipe tears off my face, he is gone forever.

I am standing alone on the spine of Sel Souris. Purple light beckons me out to the source of it. It has been calling me for years now.

I walk up the peninsula, and I focus the kinetic energy of my footsteps into blue bolts of energy that pierce the soil and seek the heart of this thing. I walk three steps, and am in New York City. The smell hits me across the face wet, and suddenly cold, and I walk three steps in Manhattan and I am back on the spine, feeling engines awaken.

I walk two steps and I am in Minneapolis and two more and I am on the spine. I feel myself in a moment back home, warm and safe, and then the salt takes me back to the spine.

The light is pulsing, and I call it up from the deep. I feel the pink and purple light hook itself in my skin and download me.

"Wake up," I tell it, "Wake up and go home."

The island shakes, and lifts and in this moment I feel the air begin to turn. Reality becomes multiple choice, and I choose to go home.

Sel Souris chooses to go home, too.

And then, it never was.

Laird Ryan States

We are in the dark together falling. Gravity is our only sense of direction, as we move to something distant and immense that calls for us. In passing we feel the drawing green warmth of something young and not alone. We turn away this time. Such bright and heavy worlds are not where we belong. We seek the union at the center of dark places. Others as immense, not fragmented, beings.

Sel Souris returns to the deep well of Home. I wake up, with a dog beside me, his pink tongue lapping at my face, his eyes fixed on mine with a desire for play. I kiss his forehead, right between the eyes in the notch that the world designed just for that purpose, and I cry.

Real again.

It is days before I really come to understand what's happened. If I even understand it now.

Sel Souris is gone.

But so too is my credit card debt gone.

And so much pain.

I don't know why.

I don't want to know why.

I'm home. I'm loved.

It's a happy ending.

And thank you for noticing.

Back in the world now, I am posting on the blogs. I am trying to conjure it back.

I post the first blog entry. I don't think that anyone will think it's factual, whatever that means, anymore. It's not even my intent that anyone does. I am writing down this dream, shaping the fragments of memory into tangible form. My real life is twisted all through the narrative.

When I realize that some people are believing in it so far, I am delighted. Not because I'm putting anything over, but because I want it to be real. I want to breathe it to life. I want my brother and his family and all of it to be real. I am writing a pastiche now, of Burroughs, and Vonnegut, and of myself and the other world that gives it life is coming real. As real as the purple light along the spine of the island.

As days pass, people start to twig to the fact that this trip never happened, I am pleased that they play along with this game.

Some people write me asking what's up. G asks me if I'm aware how many people are asking her if I've snapped.

I smile.

I've never felt more sane.

Sel Souris is a gift.

I've been waiting for a year for this working to finish. I looked through my grimoire last night, looked at spells I'd cast, and sigils I'd sent out.

Let me share this description of a sigil from November 12, 2005.

"Please let me come to an understanding of where I come from, and make peace with my family situation."

And I wish I'd kept the sigil, but this one I burned on a purple candle.

My family has been through hell the last five years. Real horrors I don't discuss. Horrors I don't look at because there's no sensible way to deal with them but to turn off. Sel Souris has made me feel at peace after years of not dealing, and I don't know why. I don't.

I have been worried that people will be angry at me when this is over. I have been worried that it will only confirm to all of you that I am an flake.

If any of you feel this way, I'm sorry. I can only say this. Just because a thing is not factual, does not make it untrue.

I'm a magician, and I deal in narratives. Metaphor is my business. I want to build an interface between real and imagined worlds. I feel I've come very close here, and if nothing else I hope I've entertained you.

I am not done with Sel Souris. Not at all. I want to go back, and I'm hoping some of you are willing to come back with me. I will need help from you, all of you, and I'll need more than vague wishes this time.

Just because Sel Souris has rotated out of our local reality is no reason not to tie an anchor here.

I wish you all peace. I thank you for reading. I need a few days to think.